09/04   1599

who
will
tell
my
brother
?

who
will
tell
my
brother
?

Marlene Carvell

HYPERION BOOKS FOR CHILDREN

NEW YORK

Printed in the United States of America

First Edition

1 3 5 7 9 10 8 6 4 2

This book is set in 13-point Perpetua.

Library of Congress Cataloging-in-Publication Data on file.

ISBN 0-7868-0827-6

Visit www. hyperionchildrensbooks.com

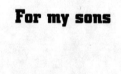

For my sons

who
will
tell
my
brother
?

When I filled out the form
for the test—
the dreaded "you will be labeled for life"
test
the "colleges will want you—or not"
test
the "who are you?—what are you?—why are you?"
test,

I wrote my name.
I wrote where I lived.

I stopped.

I did not know the answer.

Who was I?
What was I?

I went to my mother who always had the
        answers
but this time she did not have the answers.
She said the answers had to be my answers—
my answers.

I did not like the question
and although
I did not have to answer
this question
I needed to know the answer.

And so I searched my soul
and searched my past
and placed the X slowly
in the spot
which spun me on
my path in life.

♦ ♦ ♦ ♦ ♦ ♦

September 5: First Day

The beginning of the end.

As I walk alone through the halls,
I search quickly for familiar eyes,
eager to rekindle friendships
strained by summer separation,
eager to see who had returned
changed and yet unchanged,
taller and stronger and tanner
and yet the same.

Summer in the country
means long gaps of loneliness
from school-formed friendships
and though there is no
best friend waiting in the hall,
return to fall means old companions
with common ground
seeking each other out.

As I turn at the corner
of the west wing, I see
Jason Michaels and Richard Green,
fellow seniors, leaning against the lockers
looking smug.

"Hi, Evan," they holler
as I near them both;
"long time no see," they chime
together, almost in unison,
offering a token of friendship
in their greeting, letting me know
that I am one of them.

And as we three together stand
in a circle formed along the wall,
a figure passes behind and brushes
against me closely. A hand sweeps
up and pulls my hair, ever so slightly.

And as I wheel around, a laughing
Martin Bent passes by, and in a voice
that speaks more scorn than tease
calls out an ultimatum to my name.

"You oughta get it cut, Evan,
you really oughta get it cut."

♦ ♦ ♦ ♦ ♦ ♦ ♦ ♦ ♦ ♦

September 19: Birthday

I was born.
My mother says
I was a surprise
because when I was born
I looked like her.

She thought I would look like my brother—
my brother who looks like my father
whose dark skin and black hair
look so strong,
so strong.

My father says that when my older brother
        was born,
he looked through the nursery window
and saw a wizened infant image
of his grandfather—my great-grandfather—
who had left the reservation as a young man.

My brother and I had heard the stories
for many years—
the stories of how the family name was changed,
the stories of secret trips to places unknown,
the stories that unfolded as time went on
but that had been hidden for years.
For shame? Indifference?

But I am not ashamed, and I am not indifferent.

My brother looked like this man who had
        given us
a secret past, a secret history.

But I did not look like my brother
when I was born.

♦ ♦ ♦ ♦ ♦ ♦ ♦

September 21: Heritage

We are going to the reservation
tomorrow
and I feel the excitement
building in my brain—
Searching . . . always searching for my place.

We will go with my grandfather,
as he knows the way.
With my grandfather,
who probably never went with his father,
who left there long ago.

I am going with my father
and he now with his father.

My father feels the excitement, too.
It is new and strange and curious to him.
But he belongs.
They are his family.

Are they mine, too?

♦ ♦ ♦ ♦ ♦ ♦ ♦

September 22: The Welcome

As we turn into the driveway
of the ancestral home where
my great-grandfather was born,
where his youngest sister,
my great-great-aunt Margaret,
ancient clan mother,
still lives with Uncle Andrew,
I feel the fear of failure
mounting inside my body.

Are we welcome?
Are we home?
Are we family?

She meets us at the door
and a smile spreads across her face
as she greets us warmly,
easing our nervousness as we climb
the wooden steps to the clapboard-covered
cabin that holds our family's history.

We are welcome.
We are home.
We are family.

♦ ♦ ♦ ♦ ♦ ♦

September 23: Family

I met family yesterday.
New family . . .

Aunt Margaret—a fragile wisp of ancient
history whose heart is warm and open—
who understands and accepts,
she understands family,
she accepts family.
She accepts me.

Aunt Margaret—who shared with us
such memories that filled
our heads and hearts
with a sense of who we were
and who we are
and who we could become.

And Uncle Andrew—proudly serene,
sitting in his wicker chair, taking in a scene

that seemed perhaps perplexing as he
understands so little English, speaking
only Mohawk and so not speaking much at all
to us, we who could not understand,
and yet watching all before him
with a slight smile in his eyes which
made me wonder what he thought,
perhaps wondering why we had come,
perhaps questioning why.
But I knew why we had come.
We had come to find family.
And we did.

♦ ♦ ♦ ♦ ♦

September 28: School Spirit

I walk into the gym
and feel the excitement
as students sporting their class colors
fill the stands,
the air steaming with sweaty bodies
from the spirit-filled day.

I cheer with my fellow students,
cheer aimlessly, but with a fervor
that makes no sense to anyone,
but that grows in our mad passion
to win the spirit stick that passes
from year to year at homecoming.

And then a lump in my throat grows as
I glance down from the highest point in
        the stands
to the polished wooden floor below
and see the girls, young and pretty,

silly, inane, young girls in their short skirts
prancing, dancing—up and down.

But it is not their prettiness
or pep-rally prancing
that hold my view,
my view that glazes over as I stare
and the lump in my throat grows large.

I am drawn to their faces,
which are covered with streaks
of red and yellow paint.

I am drawn to their hair, pretty
blond, black, brown, bobbing hair
with colored bands around their brows
and feathers mounted atop their heads,
colored, paper feathers
listing sadly to the side.

I suck in slowly,
breathing in and out, in and out,
with teeth and hands clenched in response,
as my brain teems with confusion
and my eyes search for answers,
looking for those who also see the shame
and seeing no one.

And then the laughter loud and long
combines with war whoops echoing,
echoing through the room
as Silas McAllister stumbles
side to side in mock Indian dancing,
weaving in and out of prancing girls,
cardboard cutout hatchet
raised high above his head.

With scalping motion,
he leaps forward
toward the cheering crowd,
scowling fiercely, then whooping,
as he mounts, in short strides,
the wooden bleacher seats
to take his position high above the floor,
folding arm over arm across his chest
in proud position—
the noble savage watching
as the pretty girls with bobbing hair,
blond, black, brown, bobbing hair
with colored bands around their brows
and feathers mounted atop their heads,
move forward toward the crowd.

And as they prance throughout the stands,
placing brightly colored paper bands upon
        the heads

of laughing, cheering students,
I feel myself cringing backward, trying to melt
into the wall behind me, a wall of
ignorance, whose concrete barrier
makes me face this shame.

When Lisa Kendall reaches
the row below me, I shake my head
to show the hope I have, that she will
move away from me and leave me be.
But in one swift and thoughtless move,
she plops a paper headdress on my head
and prances off.

I lift my right hand slowly to my head
and slide the paper shame away
and crush it at my side,
letting it fall between the bleacher seats
to the floor below.

As I sit with my hands clenched
and my eyes burning, I search for comfort,
looking for those who also see the shame
and seeing no one—
except perhaps
for Maggie Brenden, who,
as she turns to clap and cheer
at Silas in his savage stance,

catches my eyes and holds them
in her gaze.

And her hands fall silent.

And in her eyes a question comes.

But then she turns away as Silas,
with cardboard cutout hatchet
raised high above his head,
swoops between us,
whooping cries of war,
flailing through the air
in leaps and bounds
downward to the floor.

♦ ♦ ♦ ♦ ♦ ♦ ♦ ♦ ♦

October 1: Search for Help

I take a deep breath
and swallow silently
before exhaling slowly
as I sit outside the office door,
trying to wait patiently,
an outward appearance of calm
as inwardly the turmoil churns.

And then the knob turns
and the door opens slowly
and a round face appears,
perched above the striped necktie
knotted tightly at the throat
of a pale blue shirt.
The face smiles broadly—
too broadly.

"Mornin'. Come on in," the voice
booms in false friendly manner,

the sound of one who tries to play
the role of principal turned friend,
but who wears his shallowness
on his sleeve like a piece of lint—
often hard to see but always there.

As I stand to enter through
the office door, I reach up and
push the hair back from my face,
wishing I had tied it behind,
suddenly aware how my long hair
separates me,
suddenly aware how important it is
for me to seem like my classmates.

But it is too late.

"So, Evan, what's on your mind?"
the voice continues as its owner
settles into the cushioned chair
behind the heavy metal desk.

I sit down slowly on the
thick wooden chair in front
and watch carefully as
he eyes me suspiciously.

I inhale deeply through my nose

and clear my throat and wonder
if my nervousness shows through
and think it likely does, since my hands
begin to shake as I hold them in my lap.

And so, with hands folded together
in false security, I begin.

"I'd like to discuss the pep rally, sir,
and our mascot." I try to sound firm,
yet friendly.

But as my plea unfolds,
I watch the figure sitting
miles across the metal desk from me
fold inward, one arm crossing over the other,
jaw setting firmly in place; eyes, cold and hard,
looking squarely into my own.

"Haven't we been here once before?"

The voice, cold and hard, speaks
volumes in its tone.

"Was this not settled
when your brother broached
this course and clearly saw
that it was not the time nor place

to champion a cause
that no one wanted?"

"But—"

"And have you not
learned anything from him,
that students here are proud
of what they are and plan to keep that pride,
as proud, perhaps, or more than
either you or Jacob think you are?"

"But—"

"It's over, Evan. It's over."

And I barely have begun
to share my thoughts,
to show my heart,
to ask for help.
His truth comes crashing down,
crushing me with its cruel limbs,
and I feel entangled in a mass of myths.

With a heavy heart I leave the room,
and as I move slowly away,
passing me in the narrow hallway
just outside the office door

is Martin Bent, eyebrows
raised in curiosity.
And though he has no sense
of what has just transpired,
there is no doubt that Martin Bent
knows something is amiss.

♦ ♦ ♦ ♦ ♦ ♦ ♦ ♦ ♦ ♦

October 3: Reflection

I look into the mirror that sits atop
the oak chest of drawers in my room—
a dresser crammed with as many memories
of long ago as it is with T-shirts and socks,
a piece of furniture with much history.
And I wonder about my own history.
I wonder who I am.

I see blue eyes set in a pale skin
framed by brown hair
that flows past my shoulders,
long hair that sets me apart
from my peers in Samson-like fashion.

And I think back to the early morning
conversation with Martin Bent
as we stood side by side at our lockers.

"Hey, Evan, if you're an Injun,
how come you don't look like one?"

He took me by surprise, as
Martin Bent and I have rarely spoken
face to face, and Martin Bent and I
see little eye to eye;
what I have often praised, he seems
to value less and less. The sole
thing we two share, perhaps,
is that our older brothers
were as different as we two.
And though the question caught me
momentarily off guard,
I suspected it was through
his older brother that Martin knew
my heritage was more than
what my skin and eyes revealed.

I turned the knob to right and left
and right, slowly, carefully,
waiting for the click,
then lifting the latch that unlocked
the gray metal door, wishing I could unlock
the door that seals in ignorance.

"What does an Injun look like, Martin?"

"You know, black hair in braids,
red skin; you know, stuff like that."

Peering intently into the darkness

of my locker, I assumed the guise of
looking for a needed book or pen while
my mind searched for a calm response.

"I guess I look like my mother, Martin."

And alone in my room
as I stare at the reflection before me,
I wonder why the color of our
skin and eyes and hair,
why the shape of a forehead—
or nose or chest—
should determine who we are,
should determine what we are.

I look into the mirror and into my soul
and I know that my strength comes not
from how I look, but how I feel—
and how I feel determines who I am.

◆ ◆ ◆ ◆ ◆ ◆ ◆ ◆ ◆ ◆ ◆ ◆ ◆

October 13: The Hand of Love

Looking at the pictures
spread out before us,
pictures taken on our journey north,
my father and I sift through them,
a sea of memories floating
on the wooden butcher block
of the cluttered kitchen counter.
I notice a similarity here and there:
a familiarity around the eyes,
a closeness to the smile,
a likeness in the shape of chin
or cheeks or brow.
Pictures spread out before us,
expanding and connecting a family,
connected by blood, yet separated
by time and distance.

Pictures of a motley clan of
short, tall, fat, thin, dark, light people

pushing together to fit into one small
frame outlined by the camera's edge,
with arms around each other
in firm familial friendship,
standing before the great river
that divides one country from another,
but not one people from another.

Looking at the pictures
spread out before us,
I notice how my father looks
long and hard at each one,
examining every detail,
reliving every captured moment
of a day spent bridging a gap
in his history and mine,
reconnecting a generation
that his father and grandfather
allowed to be eroded.

One picture stands out
among the others, stands out to
show the closeness, the acceptance,
the bond of newfound family:
Great-aunt Margaret and my grandfather,
sitting side by side on white wicker,
sitting with backs straight, framed by
the graying clapboards of the enclosed porch,

sitting full-face front with me on one side
and my father on the other.
My father smiles and slides the picture
across the counter to give me a clearer view.

"She will help you remember who you are,"
he says quietly as he taps the picture
with his fingers.

Almost unnoticed, and quite unremembered,
Aunt Margaret's ancient, wrinkled hand,
a hand worn well by work and care,
a hand lined heavily with history,
rests lovingly on top of my own.

♦ ♦ ♦ ♦ ♦ ♦ ♦ ♦ ♦ ♦ ♦ ♦

October 14: The Legacy

Alone in my room,
sitting cross-legged on my bed
in my usual working pose,
I lift my pen and begin to draw
the image in my head,
an image of hands,
proud hands, gentle hands,
wrinkled, but not withered hands,
one folded over another in solemnity.

The lines unfold on the paper before me
as my artist brain takes over
and my hand begins to move
seemingly uncontrolled,
sketching methodically,
but urgently, as though the image
might melt at any moment.
The image begins to take shape:
line upon line upon line;
lines curved and soft on the edges;

lines thick and heavy on the tops;
the palms never showing;
palms hidden from the view of the world,
hiding the worry and work of the world,
long, thin, ancient hands,
resting right upon left in peaceful harmony.

But my hands work fast and furiously,
left adjusting the paper continuously,
right gripping the pen firmly as it moves
mysteriously on its own across the paper
to capture this image held in my head,
this image of hands that hold a history;
and in each line that I draw,
I see a moment of that history
that has been shared with me,
and with each stroke of my pen
I relive a moment of the stories told
that gave her a history and that now
become a part of my own.

I see the hand of a little child who waves
to an older brother as he leaves the reservation—
an older brother whom I have come to know
as my great-grandfather, an older brother
that she remembers only in shadowy memory,
but memory that gives to me a person,
a person instead of just a picture.

I see the hand of the young girl who waves
to her father as she, at fourteen, boards the train
to go to the Indian school far away from home,
a distant place where she will learn—
a place away from home. For near her home,
there is no place in the outside world,
the white world, where she is welcome.
And so she leaves her family
to go to an Indian school.

I see the hand of a young woman who waves
in greeting to her mother as she returns
to the reservation, educated, articulate,
skilled in English, ready to reclaim
her place in her own culture.

I see the hand of the young bride who waves
to her husband as he leaves their home,
like so many, a steel construction worker,
        to climb and raise the buildings
        of the outside world,
wondering when and if she will join him,
wondering why this has to be the way.

I see the hand of a mother who waves
to her youngest son, the one
whose picture has hung high on the wall
above her favorite chair near sixty years,
a son who walked off to war never to return,

a son who could have chosen not to serve,
but saw the need and did.

I see the hand of an old woman who waves
at the door as we leave from our visit,
a woman whose warm and welcoming
hand took hold of my father's arm
during our visit and told him how he
reminded her of her brother, how he
looked and moved like the older brother
who was a shadowy memory for her
and how that shadowy memory had,
for her, once more become a person.

And with a final stroke the sketch is done.

And so I pause to view these loving hands,
a portrait of her history and of mine,
a legacy from her to me for her;
and feeling quite content and quite secure,
for like these hands my world is taking shape,
I once more lift my pen,
and just below the wrist of the left hand,
I boldly sign my name:

Evan Hill

◆ ◆ ◆

October 24: Newspaper Meeting

"You gotta be kidding,"
Samuel Patterson responds in disbelief,
tapping the ends of his fingers
on the keyboard before him,
avoiding contact with my eyes.
"Why would we want to do that?"

"It's time," I urge, "it's time."

Frances Downey peers over her
wire-framed glasses perched
on the edge of her editorial nose,
playing the role of one who longs to look
like one of intellect. She scoffs lightly,
not so much at me as at the plan I place
before the staff who, busy with their tasks,
have little time to entertain a cause.

"But, Evan, that was done before.

In fact, wasn't it your brother who
when he was here took on that charge
and found it didn't work?"

And it is true that Jacob had,
in fact, begun some time ago
what now I see is still a cause
that cries for confirmation,
and in my heart I know that
it is time to make that change.

When Samuel stops his work
and turns to see me face to face,
the others all pause,
waiting as he sighs and groans,
waiting patiently for his thoughts.

"Your brother tried and failed," he says,
"and though you think the time is right
to change this mascot we've had for years,
are you prepared for what you know,
for what I know, for what everyone here knows
will occur?"

"But all I ask is that we try,"
I offer once again, hiding my
anger that he should think that
Jacob failed. My brother did not fail;

he only started what has not been finished.

I know they do not disagree,
but neither do they understand
that this is not some idle cause.
And so when Frances Downey nods
vaguely in assent, I feel a glint of hope
and reach into the empty air,
offering a plan, a thought,
a course of action
we could take together.

Proposal after proposal falls,
not so much on deaf ears,
as on indifferent ones, a small group
of listeners who care little either way:
they are not filled with vacant pride over an
Indian face that supposedly serves
to spur us on in our high school endeavors,
nor are they imbued with a sense of justice
for a culture they do not embrace.

Richard Green, my childhood friend
and sometime confidant, looks up
from the table where, hard at work,
he proofs the page before him.
I implore him silently to offer his support,
but when he sees my eyes on his,

my heart and hope both fall;
he shrugs his shoulders
and shakes his head.

"No point, Evan."

No point?

And now I know
that I am all alone.

♦ ♦ ♦ ♦ ♦ ♦ ♦

November 13: Plea for Justice

My heart pounds as I carefully examine
the sea of faces before me, all smiling,
some friendly, some patronizing,
all wondering why I am here,
wondering why I have come
to this school board meeting,
men and women elected by the community
to make the decisions that guide our school.

I glance to my right,
assured by my father's presence.
I am not alone.

This sea of faces looks at me inquisitively,
patiently waiting to know why I have come.

And the knot in my stomach grows tighter.

My brother, years before,
stood in this same place,

with a different sea of faces,
but with the same intent.

And so I begin my plea,
a request for honor,
for dignity,
a request to remove an injustice,
a request to remove a face—
an Indian face—from our walls,
our fields, our banners,

a request to remove an injustice,
an attitude,
from our minds,
our hearts,
our souls.

As I speak, I see the sea of faces
clouding over, mouths tightening,
eyes staring blankly at the back wall.

I feel my stomach tighten,
but I hear my father's breath,
drawn in deeply and exhaled slowly
as though he were transferring his
strength, his power, his being, to me.

And I continue.

But the reality becomes clear,
the reality my brother saw years before,
the reality my mother and my father
warned would be.

Erasing a picture is easy;
Erasing an attitude is not.

♦ ♦ ♦ ♦ ♦ ♦ ♦ ♦ ♦

November 21: Love

I look out the window
and see the car easing slowly into the driveway,
moving cautiously up the gravel path.

My brother is home for the holiday.

And although I recognize the car,
I know it cannot be my brother driving,
since my brother Jacob
never moves cautiously anywhere.
As the green Ford rolls to a stop
just beyond the back steps,
I see Mary Alice lean back in the driver's seat,
and turn her head slowly toward the house,
waiting as always to see if Butch will come
bounding up, barking territorially,
ready to defend our home, our honor, our lives.

And before I barely exit the kitchen door,
Jacob leaps from the car

and, protecting his love from this
demon wimp of a dog, throws his arms
about Butch's neck and presses his face
into the soft fur.

And Butch, full of love for his boy,
forgets the threat of Mary Alice—
her love for Jacob and his for her—
and nuzzles his face into Jacob's chest.

"Hey, ol' boy," Jacob murmurs,
momentarily caught in the past,
in a time when dog and boy greeted
each other daily.

I know that Jacob worries
Butch will forget him
and a part of his childhood
will be gone forever,
or, worse, fears when Butch
will not be there at all.

I stand on the brick walk
and watch this scene with envy.

When Jacob left for college,
so many hours away, Butch
looked longingly up the gravel drive for days,
wondering, waiting.

And though I gave the usual greeting,
"Hey, ol' boy," 'most every day,
Butch would view me with disdain and
back away as though I had interfered
with some arcane ritual held
for him and Jacob alone.

"Hello, Evan."

Mary Alice, having magically
moved from the driver's seat,
stands beside me,
she, too, looking down on the
scene before us.

"We've been replaced by a mutt,"
she laughs, and putting her arm
around my waist, we turn away
and move into the warmth of the kitchen,
escaping the autumn chill, leaving Jacob
immersed in his childhood.

"Looks like we're alone," she adds.

"Don't worry," I said.
"I'm used to it."

♦　♦　♦　♦　♦　♦

November 29: Ghosts

When the phone rang this evening,
my mother, washing dishes in the kitchen,
quickly dried her soap-sudsed hands
on the towel that hangs on the iron bar
above the sink and lifted the receiver as
the rings subsided, only to discover
my father had answered it
on the upstairs extension;
and as she returned the phone gently
to its hook, so as not to disturb the
conversation already underway,
I saw the shadow cross her face.

"Your grandfather," she responded
to my silent inquiry as I looked up
from the table where I sat sketching
with pen and ink.

My grandfather? My grandfather?
Grandfather never called.

My grandfather loved his family,
but largely ignored us, and lived an isolated life
in the foothills of the Adirondacks
where family ghosts loomed everywhere
        and nowhere,
where he, an eldest son, alone remained,
one living figure whose brothers and sons had,
like his own father, left in search of life and hope.

My grandfather? My grandfather?
Grandfather never called.

My mother continued with her task at hand,
hands once more immersed in mindless work,
though more than once she glanced at me
as I sat, paused, my pen resting idly in my hand.
And so we waited patiently
until we heard my father's footsteps
moving across the upstairs hall,
growing louder as they descended;
and as my father moved into the doorway,
his countenance confirmed our thoughts;
we only questioned who.

"Uncle Andrew has died," he said.

♦ ♦ ♦ ♦ ♦ ♦ ♦ ♦ ♦ ♦ ♦

December 1: Journey

Today my father and I
return to the reservation.
It is a long trip to have gone so
soon again.

Just my father and I, in deep,
quiet conversation all the way
north through the land so familiar
to his youth, but not to mine.

Just my father and I, as my mother
does not share her sorrow well with others.

So we come alone, we two, father and son,
in deep conversation all the way north.

I look down the narrow street
toward the red brick funeral home,
a one-story building framed with yellow trim

around the doors and windows,
and see mourners gathering on the front porch.
I glance at my father
to see if he senses my apprehension;
it seems too soon to share the sorrow
of newfound family.

We drive into the crowded parking lot
and ease slowly into the one empty space.
Uncle Andrew had much family, to leave
only one space empty.

And now we are the family
to come and fill
the empty space.

♦ ♦ ♦ ♦ ♦ ♦

December 2: It Is Important to Know Who
You Are When You Die

When we return home today,
my mother, hungry for conversation,
cannot let us rest
and showers us with questions,
worried that her absence might
make her seem uncaring.

And so we tell her of our day
and how the aunts and uncles, cousins,
close and much removed,
could not let us rest
and showered us with questions.

How their questions made us feel
warm and welcome.

How those we have known for years,
and those we have not,
all wished she had come,

but understood when we explained
she keeps her grief in private.

How we went to the church
and listened to the prayers and
songs in a language so many of us
never knew or have long forgotten.

How we all walked to the cemetery
in silent file, my father walking proudly
beside his father, who now walks
with faltering steps and stops,
pausing briefly, to catch his breath.

How we paid our respects
to Aunt Margaret who now in her
hundredth year is once again alone,
two husbands and so many of her
fifteen children leaving her in sorrow.

I am glad I went with my father
to see that Uncle Andrew's soul was put to rest.

It is important to know who you are when
you die.

♦ ♦ ♦ ♦ ♦ ♦

December 5: Friend and Foe

"Hi, Evan."

I glance up from the tray before me
to see a pair of soft green eyes
smiling in greeting,
Maggie Brenden's soft green eyes,
Maggie Brenden, who looks out for
every lost kitten and stray dog,
and for a moment I wonder
where I fit in her plan to save the world.

"I heard you went to a funeral
over the weekend," she blurts out,
plunking herself down at the
cafeteria table where I now sit alone,
Jason Michaels and Samuel Patterson
having hurried off to finish homework tasks.
"Someone close?"

Her directness surprises me

and though my inclination often is
to keep my thoughts inside, it is not in
Maggie's nature to be mean or wish one ill
and her inquiry seems thoughtful
and most certainly sincere.

"An uncle," I respond
without further explanation.

But as Maggie sits in silence,
her soft green eyes in conflict,
both watching me and glancing
surreptitiously around the room, I know
that she is looking for a moment,
a pause in our silent conversation
so she can share some thought.

"What's on your mind, Maggie?"

Her smile fades and a cloudiness
invades those soft green eyes.
"Martin, Evan. He says you're trouble."

"How so?"

"I don't think that Martin
needs a reason for his thoughts.
If Martin thinks you're trouble then,
        to Martin, you are."

And as I shrug my shoulders in response
to her concern, she rises slowly
from the bench and leans slightly forward.

"I just thought you ought to know, Evan.
I just thought you ought to know."

"Do you think I'm trouble, Maggie?"

"I think you're *in* trouble, Evan."

♦ ♦ ♦ ♦ ♦ ♦ ♦ ♦ ♦ ♦ ♦ ♦ ♦

December 11: A Second Plea

My father and I walk with confidence
into the room, surmising at once
the surprise at our presence.
I wonder if they thought
that I would not return, that my plea
was not heartfelt, that perhaps it was
the misplaced priority of a teenager
looking for a cause?

As we settle into the coldness of the room,
my father places his winter coat
on the back of the wooden chair
and as he sits down, he whispers,
"I don't think they expected you back, Evan."
He pats my left knee in affirmation
of his confidence in me.

We sit and listen, politely and patiently,
to mundane issues, to matters of business;

and then the time comes for anyone
who wishes to speak.

And so I speak.

"A month ago I came to ask your help.
I asked that you listen to my request,
and you did.
I asked that you think about what I said,
and I hope you have.
I have come again to ask
if you, as leaders of our school,
as models for my peers,
might be willing now to take action,
yes—an unpopular action,
but one which would right a wrong."

I once again express concern,
concern for more than just a picture—
an issue; a mascot; a tradition that reflects poorly
on so many cultures and so many peoples.
And I am questioned about my concern.
Do I have a right to speak
for these many cultures?
for these many peoples?

And when I claim I do,
their faces say I do not.

And when I claim I should,
their faces say I should not.

And so before I leave,
they ask for more time:
decisions should not be hasty.
They ask for more information:
decisions should be thoughtful.
They ask for my patience.

As my father starts the truck,
and the warmth from the engine
begins to fill the cab, I feel the chill
of the evening dissipate.
"They don't understand, do they?"
I ask my father as he slides the seat belt
slowly across his chest and snaps it into place.

I know my father's strength is in his calm;
He is so strong and so secure—
but tonight he said nothing.
And I am glad. I know he shares my view—
that an Indian face as a mascot for a school
creates a feeling of dishonor, not pride,
creates a sense of shame, not respect.
I am glad he comes and sits beside me—
a reminder to this Board of Education
that this disrespect goes well beyond

a student looking for a cause.

But he knows the fight is mine,
that it is part of finding my place,
of knowing who I am. And so he comes
and sits beside me and, in his silence,
speaks volumes.

"They want my patience," I scoff.

My father shifts in his seat and I know
he hears the impatience in my voice.

"Well, Evan, do you have the patience?"

"Yes," I answer, "for the moment."

♦ ♦ ♦ ♦ ♦ ♦ ♦ ♦ ♦ ♦ ♦

December 12: Patience

Silas McAllister and Martin Bent
lean lazily against the lockers
outside the English classroom,
waiting for the first period bell to ring.

As I stop at the doorway
of the room on the opposite wall
to place a homework paper
in the cardboard folder
mounted on Mrs. Brundage's door,
Martin's voice artificially rises in volume.

"Hey, Silas, I hear we got a hippie
in the school, an Injun hippie."

Silas looks at Martin vacantly,
missing the cue to taunt.
"Huh?"

Martin shrugs his shoulders

and shakes his head in annoyance
as his right hand reaches up and
raps the side of Silas's head.

"Hey," Silas yelps,
rubbing his temple, looking
somewhat like a forlorn mutt
whose master's act of love
manifests itself in abuse,
and hungry for attention
accepts what it is offered.

"An Injun hippie," Martin repeats
as he nods in my direction.

Silas slowly, slightly, understands his point.
"Huh? Oh, yeah, a hippie. We got
us a real hippie here," he responds
in a puzzled tone as I pass by,
already late for Civics.

The bell rings and Martin and Silas
slip into the classroom,
and the patience that last night
I told my father was in my grasp
slips farther and farther away.

♦ ♦ ♦ ♦ ♦ ♦ ♦ ♦ ♦ ♦ ♦

December 14: Approval

Peering down from the picture
placed high above the mantel,
where the glow of the fire softens
his portrait, he watches as I
hang the childhood stockings.
He watches every move,
and I often wonder
if he wonders who I am,
if he wonders, do I know?
Do I know of the past that he hid
from so many?
Does he know that I wonder
about him, that I wonder if he,
had times been different,
might have chosen a different course?

His dark eyes reveal my father's
likeness to him, and
I wonder if he would approve of me.

Would he approve of my course of action
as I move to end the ignorance?
Would he who hid his past approve
my public proclamation of my own?

My father enters the room
and pauses beside me, sensing
a simple task has taken far too long.

I turn as I sense his presence and
see in his eyes the eyes of his grandfather,
the eyes of someone far more patient than I.

"Evan? he inquires, our eyes linking in thought.

"Just wondering," I reply.

♦ ♦ ♦ ♦ ♦ ♦ ♦ ♦ ♦ ♦

December 22: Brothers

Jacob and I find ourselves
in heavy brother conversation,
he sitting on the floor,
back propped up against the wall,
right hand resting on Butch's head,
and me slumped over the edge of
his unmade bed. We plan our futures
as we did so many years before
when I was ten and he was twelve.
Then future meant the summer,
fifteen days away.

Home from college on holiday,
Jacob seems still so distant,
as though each time at home,
he knows the break is stronger.
He knows that soon the visits home
will be truly visits,
momentary stops on his life journey,

moments to recapture once more
the warmth of home.

Soon I, too, will be on my life journey.
Soon I will be the one who visits,
who comes, perhaps with Jacob,
two brothers off together
once more seeking home.

Perhaps it is the Christmas spirit
that sets us off on conversation,
that makes us wonder when childhood
comes to an end,
when we will have our own Christmases
in celebration elsewhere.

Perhaps it is the smell of warmed apple cider
and gingerbread wafting up the stairs that
makes us long to postpone life's decisions
until another time.

And in our heavy brother conversation,
with great relief, we recognize
that such a time is yet some time away
and so we plan our futures as though,
yet no longer ages ten and twelve,
the future is just summer—months away.

♦ ♦ ♦ ♦ ♦ ♦ ♦ ♦ ♦ ♦ ♦ ♦ ♦ ♦ ♦

December 24: The Gift

Wrapped loosely in green tissue paper
tied with red striped ribbon and solid red bow,
my present to my father rests under our tree.
It is an eight-foot Douglas fir
poised majestically
        in the corner of the living room
where my mother and I last week moved chairs
and sofa and desk and lamps,
rearranged to make way for our holiday addition;
underneath our tree rests a present
to my father, created from my soul,
a gift of his history, a gift of myself,
a gift symbolic of my commitment
to honor and dignity,
to family and future.

As we begin the ritualistic exchange
of Christmas Eve gifts, each of us choosing one
to share before our journey off to Mass,
I slide this favored gift toward my father.

"Hmm, Evan, what's this? From you?"

I nod as my brother and my mother
pause from their unwrapping of gifts,
watching my father, waiting to see
how he responds to what I have
in secret shared with them.

He carefully removes the ribbon,
setting it on the floor next to his chair,
and folds the tissue paper back,
revealing underneath, framed by rosewood
and safely protected under glass,
a pair of ancient, noble hands.

♦ ♦ ♦ ♦ ♦ ♦ ♦ ♦ ♦ ♦ ♦

January 1: Godmother

I spoke on the phone with my father.
He and my mother went to Canada
for the holidays.

They were looking for the graves of my
great-grandmother's grandparents.
My great-grandmother,
who was my godmother,
though I was too young to remember.
I only remember her from the
picture that hangs on my bedroom wall.
My great-grandmother, who married a man
who left the reservation,
who helped him keep the secret, the past hidden.
My great-grandmother,
whose name is my name,
but whose name, like her husband's,
is not her real name, but Anglicized
when her family left Canada.

And now my father,
who gives me my Mohawk roots,
is searching for the graves
of his French ancestors
who, too, lost their identity.

So many dead people

who shape our lives
and make us wonder
who we are.

♦ ♦ ♦ ♦ ♦

January 3: Namesake

My parents arrived home yesterday.
There was too much snow to find the graves
of my great-grandmother's grandparents.
They will try again in the spring.

And so I look at the picture
on my bedroom wall,
a faded photograph in black and white,
a young woman who looks
at me with her tender eyes,
this woman who gives me her name
as my name—as my middle name.
Can she be the same woman, my godmother,
old and wrinkled, with a dog in her lap
and me a toddler leaning against her knee,
in the picture on the wall downstairs?

Can she be the same woman
my father says was as tough as

leather straps soaked in water
and allowed to dry in the sun?
Can she be the same young French woman
who married the dark, handsome Mohawk man
who left the reservation?

My father says she had a harsh tongue
and a taskmaster's soul.
Perhaps years of hiding a secret
hardened her soul.

I turn away from the picture
and yet I feel her watching me.
with her tender, haunting eyes.
Does she still feel shame?
Does she know that her history
is mine?

♦ ♦ ♦ ♦

January 12: Anticipation

"It's here! It's here!" I shout
as I sweep into the kitchen, placing
the narrow white envelope on the
counter and stepping back as though
in awe of something mystical
about to happen in my world.

My father emerges from underneath
the bathroom sink where, surrounded
by tools and odd pieces of plastic pipe,
he has been making a valiant effort
at solving our most recent plumbing puzzle.

"Well, Evan?" his inquiry hinting
slightly at amusement, as though he held
the ending line to some small joke.

He knows me well and knows that,
though I've waited weeks

for just this moment,
the putting-off is part of some grand plan,
some necessary rite of passage
that has to be endured.

"Shall I wait for Mom?" I ask,
half hoping he'll say yes, but knowing
well what his response will be.

"The letter there is yours,
so you decide."

I stare as though my eyes
could pierce the paper folds,
as though, clairvoyant, I might see
my destiny planned out before me, as though,
no matter what the content of the letter says,
by wishing it I just could make it so.

And knowing how my mother would
          not mind,
as she had faith that any school, any college,
any place was mine if so I chose,
I take the letter in my hand and slit the edge
with one deft move, sliding out the single
          sheet
of paper. I read the contents slowly to myself
and then glance up to see my father,

standing there, patiently, as always,
waiting patiently for me to share.

"I'm in."

♦   ♦   ♦   ♦

January 15: Third Plea for Justice

With chairs scraping sharply
against the wooden floors
and papers rustling on the table
separating me from the wall of hardened eyes,
I know my presence is unwelcome,
not by all, but most,
and those most
are the ones
who have already dismissed my request.

My presence has been wished away
like those who have gone before me,
years past, decades past, centuries past . . .
wished away. They had hoped
I would be passionless, had hoped my plea
would be the quixotic fancy of a restless teen,
and then their own passion
would not have to be tested.

My research done, I lay before them
the histories, the data, the precedents,
but people will not listen
to what they do not want to hear;
they nod politely, even praise my efforts,
and offer shallow comments,
as if to show we share some sort of bond.

"We probably all have Indian blood,"
one voice speaks up as others nod and smile.

I offer case after case after case
where others found it hard to break tradition,
but understood and found the courage to lead.
But they will not listen
to what they do not want to hear.

"We understand, Evan, we understand.
But you must understand
this is a source of pride.
You want a world that's perfect,
one no one will understand."

And they do not understand that my plea
is not to build a utopia in this vacuum valley,
but only to move forward,
not backward, in time.
And as they grow impatient

with the present time,
it grows impossible for them
to consider the future.

Their tolerance tried and my patience ended,
I utter my final comment:

"You are trying to preserve a picture,
a false identity, an image that does not honor.
You want to maintain a sense of pride,
but by holding fast to this false identity,
you force others to lose theirs.
You force me to lose mine.
This does not honor a race—
it demeans it."

They shift restlessly in their chairs,
clearly tired of my quest. And after seconds
of uncomfortable silence, one voice speaks:

"But, Evan, racism is a matter of opinion."

Hmmm.

♦ ♦ ♦ ♦

January 16: Questioning

The word has gotten out.
The word is spreading that I have
done the unthinkable.
I have questioned
I have questioned
I have questioned why we need this mascot.

They stare at me through the cold, hard eyes
of those who feel threatened,
whose pride
whose tradition
whose bigotry
and narrow thought
is threatened.

I, too, feel threatened.

I have spoken
for those who cannot speak,

for those who have come before me
and felt threatened;
their dignity, their honor, their humanity
threatened.

I have spoken for my father and for his father
and for his father who changed his name
because he, too, felt threatened,
threatened that he could not succeed,
could not survive
unless he left the reservation
unless he changed his name
so no one would know who he was.

And so I have questioned why.
Why does our school need the face of an Indian
hanging on a wall, stitched on a shirt,
     emblazoned on a hat?
Why do we need that face to know who we are?

♦ ♦ ♦ ♦ ♦ ♦ ♦ ♦ ♦ ♦ ♦ ♦ ♦ ♦ ♦ ♦ ♦ ♦ ♦

January 23: Rights

After third period and before the bell for fourth
begins to ring, Silas McAllister slides in step
beside me as we both move quickly
through the hall together, heading
toward the same classroom. Silas,
classmate since the early grades, thinks
he knows me well, and I him, and often
thinks he is my friend.
But he is not.
He thinks I am immune to hurt.
But I am not.

"Hey, Evan, Martin says we got the right
to use whatever we want for our mascot.
It's in the Constitution. We got the right.
How come you say we got no right?"

"No, Silas, I never said you have no right."

"But Martin says you said we don't."

I pause and sigh, and Silas stops
beside me in the hall.

"Of course you have the right."

"We do?"

As we stand face to face,
I look into his eyes and think—
Oh, Silas, how obtuse you are.
But as I speak, I choose my words
to play with Silas's mind.

"You have the right, Silas,
you have the right.
When the progenitors of this country
coalesced the philosophies of ancestral nations,
and intertwined new theories on human rights,
a document created gave citizens
the right to speak, to think, to be.
And so, yes, you have the right."

And Silas, in his familiar glazed manner,
just looks at me, uncomprehending.

"We do?"

"You have the right, Silas,

not to sit beside William Mullen."
William Mullen whose black skin both
helps and hurts him in a world where
claiming to be his friend allows for affirmation
of one's tolerance, but watch
and wait and see
how shallow that friendship is when
William Mullen truly needs a friend.

"You have the right, Silas,
to not be friends with Joseph Steinman."
Joseph Steinman who, with his parents,
must travel miles and miles to worship,
and whose absence on a holy day is noted
with resentment and cynicism.

"You have the right, Silas,
to march with Thomas Allen."
Thomas Allen, self-proclaimed neo-Nazi,
who with his small band of followers,
plays the role of quasi-terrorist,
working, he says, to affirm the
future of a decent society.

"You have the right, Silas,
to avoid Roberta Bell."
Roberta Bell, who in her sophomore year
announced that she was gay

and shocked the Thomas Allens
with her beautiful prom date.

"You have the right, Silas."

You have the right.

How sad that Silas wants the right.

♦ ♦ ♦ ♦ ♦ ♦ ♦ ♦ ♦ ♦ ♦ ♦ ♦

February 11: Reality

In history class, the buzzing
stops as soon as I enter,
the chitchat among friends,
sharing thoughts before a class begins,
comes to an abrupt halt
and classmates,
former friends and newfound enemies,
stare stolidly into their notebooks,
isolating themselves from the tension
that has become prevalent with my presence.

I take my place,
third row, second seat,
take my place behind Lisa Kendall,
Lisa Kendall who turns and smiles,
flashing her hazel eyes.

"Evan?" Her voice lifts softly
at the end of my name. "Evan, is it

true you are an Indian . . . a real Indian?"
She flashes her smile again and brushes her
reddish-brown hair from her forehead,
waiting for my reply.

I pause patiently; I have become used
to the questions, the often cruel,
often benign questions, the questions
fueled by ignorance,
intolerance,
impatience.

What does she want me to say?
What does she want to hear?
I search for answers and, like a phoenix,
those answers rise from the ashes of my soul.

I am a real everything.
I am a real American,
a real Frenchman,
a real Englishman,
a real Mohawk,
a real male, a real teenager, a real Catholic,
a real brother, a real son, a real person.

"No, Lisa, there are no real Indians."

"Oh," Lisa says, tossing her hair

as she turns back in her seat.
"I didn't think so."

And though the buzzing in the class has stopped,
I feel the buzzing in my head begin.

♦ ♦ ♦ ♦ ♦ ♦ ♦ ♦ ♦ ♦ ♦ ♦ ♦ ♦ ♦

February 12: Stupidity

"So, if you don't like it here,
why don'tcha go away?" Martin Bent
questions on the way to physics.

Martin Bent, whose alcoholic father,
      Martin Bent,
beats his son—
beats him with words, and
hands thick from work in the fields,
on the farm that Martin will
one day own and work.
Someday Martin's hands
will become thick. Will Martin
have hands that will beat his son,
Martin Bent?

"Yeah," Silas snarls from behind Martin,
curling his lips in his usual way,
mouth slightly open, teeth together,

much like an angry barn cat
whose domain is threatened;
"Yeah," he snarls again,
"why don'tcha go away. Why don'tcha
go back where ya came from? You
and all them other Injuns. Go back
where ya came from."

Ignorant bastard.

♦ ♦ ♦ ♦ ♦ ♦ ♦

February 13: Fear

Behind me in the hall
I hear the grunting noises
and as I turn, a body sweating
from the heat of hate, and fear, and cruelty
sweeps by me.

"Mornin', Injun."

And now in afternoon,
the subtle grunts that greeted me
as I moved quietly through the morning halls
turn into war whoops, but quiet whoops from
those who know that what they do is cruel.

But cruelty is what they know.

They do not know who they are.

And they are afraid they will lose a tradition

that helps them know who they are—
or who they think they are.

They think a picture painted on a wall
proclaims their pride,
assures them they have tradition,
and tradition must be respected.

They think they are tolerant.

The mascot for our school
was once a whooping cartoon figure—
a scowling face and menacing eyes
frozen in a leap with hatchet
held high above the head.
And so they covered up intolerance
with a mascot that has now become
a face with hollow eyes and hook nose,
a face adorned with the feathered headdress
of a tribe that never knew the soil of here;

and now, they say we have
a noble face
a worthy face
a face that means respect.

And so, the war whoops—
the underbreath, subtle war whoops

that follow me through the halls
must be signs of respect.

And so I am respected, but the respect
is shown in fear and hate and cruelty.

And they feel secure in their tradition.

And I feel no respect.

♦ ♦ ♦ ♦ ♦ ♦ ♦ ♦ ♦

February 14: Valentine Friendship

As I close my locker, the clang of metal
against metal echoes through the hall,
reverberating in the emptiness
of after school.
And as I turn, I am startled
by a slim figure
standing behind me,
silently, serenely.

And as I turn, her outstretched arm
places a single white rose
into the palm of my hand.

A white rose of friendship, offered to me
by a childhood schoolmate, a classmate
who has watched in silent support
and now steps forward to be my friend.

"What's this?" I ask.

"A peace offering," Maggie replies.

I could use some peace.

♦ ♦ ♦ ♦ ♦ ♦ ♦ ♦ ♦ ♦

February 15: Chant

One little, two little
three little insults;
four little, five little
six little insults;
seven little, eight little,
nine little insults,
ten little insults more.

Four war hoops, five *ughs* plus
one tomahawk chop
all came on this Monday;
not likely to stop.

Six chants, seven *Hows* came
on Tuesday this week
and war whoops galore from
the freaks who don't speak.

Eight war whoops, nine *ughs*—

It's always the same;
all Wednesday long
I put up with this game.

I came to be known as
both Tonto and Chief,
but Thursday a flower
gave me some relief.

And now it is Friday,
I long to go home.
It's tough being noble
when you're all alone.

♦ ♦ ♦ ♦ ♦ ♦ ♦ ♦ ♦

February 16: The Plunge

Looking down from the top of the slope,
I take a deep breath in and see before me
a sea of hills and valleys, covered in shadows
from the nearly setting sun, shadows that
plunge the world into purpleness.

"Race ya, Evan."

I glance over my shoulder and see
Jason Michaels has slid up close beside me;
Jason, who sits next to me in physics class
and asks on every test how I have scored,
now longs for further competition,
but one of friendliness, to test our strength,
our speed, our snowy-mountain mettle.

I reach up and pull my goggles down,
casting the world below me further into shadow
as I sweep over the edge, skis straight,

eyes forward, leaving behind all hesitation.

As the world blurs by,
my body effortlessly sails
down through the snow, as though
my skis skim over this snowy cloud
in quiet, surreal fashion. And in my mind's eyes
I see other skiers, floating peripherally
off to right and left, but never down below me;

and all sense of space below me disappears,
and there I am, left in blurry whiteness,
and there I was, within the snowy fog.

And then I am alone, alone, alone.
But it is a quiet loneliness,
a welcome loneliness,
a safe loneliness.

"Race ya, Evan."

And then,
I reach up and pull my goggles down
as I sweep over the edge.

♦ ♦ ♦ ♦ ♦ ♦ ♦ ♦ ♦ ♦

February 19: Fourth Plea for Justice

Once more I approach the board;
once more I ask for reason;
once more I hear their empty reasons,
their lack of tolerance and understanding.

But this time their words
are harsh and clear
and the meaning is not misunderstood:

"Racism is a matter of opinion."

♦ ♦ ♦ ♦ ♦ ♦ ♦ ♦ ♦ ♦ ♦ ♦

February 20: Pals

"Evan, hey, Evan!"
Silas, sliding up beside me,
on the way to physics, once again asks,
"Why don'tcha move if ya don't like it here?"

And as I stare blankly at Silas,
I hear echoes from the night before
and reality passes before my eyes:
ignorance and intolerance are passed on
from one generation to another.

At last night's meeting a generation of adults
who say they speak for our community
treated me as though I were an outsider,
as though this were not my community,
as though I were someone
who had not been born here,
and had no right to speak because my parents
had not been born here.

They spoke as though the school were theirs,
       not ours.

Why do they not want to accept that I
       am from here,
that I am part of here as much as I am a part of
my heritage from elsewhere?

Why do they want to separate me?
Why do they presume I speak, not from
       my heart,
but from some misdirected cause?
Why do they not want to see that I
am proud of my school and my home
and that is why I do not want it shamed
by a tradition long past its time?

And as Silas and I enter the classroom,
the reality echoes in my head—
the reality that Silas is only an echo.
I turn to Silas and, with a broad smile, say,
"But, Silas, what would you do without
       me around?"

"Huh?" Silas responds, caught off guard.

"You and me are pals, Silas," I say
as I put my arm around his muscled shoulder.

"You and me, you and me are in this together.
They can't do this to us!"

And Silas backs away,
suspicious of my sudden friendship,
suspicious that an unwelcomed, unexpected
bond has been implied,
and not knowing how to respond,
his bluster falls apart
and, momentarily, I have peace.

♦ ♦ ♦ ♦ ♦ ♦ ♦ ♦ ♦ ♦ ♦ ♦

February 21: Pride Cometh Before a Fall

Mrs. Brundage—
tall, stern, ancient Mrs. Brundage—
pulls me aside today
in the hall outside her room
and, in concealed whispers,
tells me she is proud of me.
"It is good to know someone who
believes in what he is doing,
who knows morality and recognizes injustice,
who understands conviction and is willing
to take the risks of alienation."

She certainly is right about that.
I am alienated.

But I am perplexed by her comments
and her observations:
I am not *willing* to take the risks
of which she spoke.

I simply have no choice.

My destiny has been laid out
before me like topographical
maps of a Mount Everest climb.
Once I have started my ascent,
the collapsing snow bridges
allow for no turning back.

I have no choice.

As I listen to her words
of encouragement, spoken softly
in whispered tones lest someone overhear,
I hear the hollowness of her own convictions.

"I am proud of you, Evan."

And as I stand listening,
she glances up and down the hall,
vigilant, guarded,
fearful of falling into the crevasse
of her own collapsed snow bridge.

I wish I could be proud of her,
but I cannot.

♦ ♦ ♦ ♦ ♦ ♦

February 27: Hides His Smile

I look at the blank paper before me,
thinking about the poem Mrs. Brundage
has assigned for English tomorrow.
I have put it off and put it off
and tomorrow will soon be here.
I am an artist, not a writer.

She said we should write about ourselves,
describe one feature that makes us special.
Perhaps I should write about my long hair
but it has not made me special.
It has made me different.

"Evan," my mother calls softly as she
raps lightly on my bedroom door.

"Come in," I say.

"Homework done?"

I lift the empty paper off my desk
and wave it in the air.

"No," I respond sourly.

"My, my," she teases.
"It can't be that bad. Smile."

And though she knows my sneer
is not sincere, I glower at her
till she backs away and leaves me
to my misery.

I do not want to smile.

My mother used to say my smile
was very special—
special because I did not let
many people see it. But when I did,
they would say how wonderful it was.
My father used to say
that I did not have an Indian name,
but if I did, it would be Hides His Smile.

I pick up my pen and begin to write.

♦ ♦ ♦ ♦ ♦ ♦ ♦ ♦ ♦ ♦ ♦ ♦ ♦

March 2: Portrait

I walk softly through the room,
the stillness sealing in the night,
as my mother, settled into the corner chair
with Butch firmly planted at her feet,
looks up from her concentration
and motions for me to join her.

I settle down slowly onto the arm of her chair
and she sweeps her hand over a picture
in the album resting in her lap.

It is a picture I have seen many times before,
but one I now view with a new vision.
This portrait of the man before me who has been
only an ancestor from a time past memory
now speaks loudly and clearly through his visage.

Here is a countenance from a time past,
from this century and last,

a father to my grandfather's father,
a leader for his land,
a chief for his people—for our people.

He wears no headdress,
no feathers,
no buckskin breeches
or leather leggings.

He sports no headband,
carries no hatchet,
wears no war paint.

This image before me,
a suited man in shirt and tie,
with soft, tired eyes,
looks proudly into the camera.

But he does not smile.

"Well, Evan," my mother asks.
"What do you think?"

I think he looks like me.

♦ ♦ ♦ ♦ ♦ ♦ ♦ ♦ ♦

March 4: Isolation

I walk down the hall
feeling the pressure build inside me
as my smear-spattered locker
comes into view.

A glob of ugly spit splattered
eye level confronts me full-face,
oozing slowly downward.

Do I tell? Do I tell?

Who will listen?

As I walk slowly to the boys' room,
I feel the eyes watching me,
boring into my brain,
trying to see my thoughts,
waiting and watching
to see my course of action.

I take the brown paper and wipe the smear
from the cold, hard surface of my locker
and into my heart.

♦ ♦ ♦ ♦ ♦ ♦ ♦

March 7: Comfort

Today I felt the cold hard stares.
My mother says I must not care . . .
but I care.

But when I came home
she saw the tears welling in my
eyes and held me
close to her heart.

As her arms swept around my chest,
she leaned against me,
head to heart
warmth to warmth.

As I looked down
on my mother's head,
she who could look down on mine
not so long ago
felt my hurt, knew my pain.

My mother says I must not care . . .
but I know
she cared.

♦ ♦ ♦ ♦

March 12: Another Plea

Petulant voices murmur
in hushed tones.
The wooden chairs scrape
across the cold linoleum floor.
We take our seats, my father
and I, and now my mother,
in the front of the room,
facing this wall of brows
as all heads bend downward,
poring over the papers before them,
avoiding our eyes.

The message is given
unspoken, unvoiced,
unwarranted: *Unwanted!*
Frustration the month before
has fermented, and I see
before me a churning cauldron
of annoyance turning to anger.

Their chairs shuffle restlessly,
as I begin to speak again,
again my plea,
my hope
that they might set a standard
of tolerance by removing
this face which affronts.

But it is they who
are affronted by my plea.

Their time is important, and
they have heard all this before.
Is this new information?
Is it truly important?

♦ ♦ ♦ ♦ ♦ ♦ ♦ ♦

March 20: Creativity

I walk into the art studio,
heading toward my solitude,
an area claimed by senior status
and earned through dedication.
It is a work space that is solely mine,
littered with paints and pencils,
oak tag and parchment,
charcoal and canvas.

As I approach this corner of creativity,
I nonchalantly touch the keyboard
of the computer where, deeply engrossed,
day after day, I have labored over one project
after another. And as the waving geometric
pattern vanishes from the screen,
my eyes focus unexpectedly
on a tomahawk, dripping with blood,
held high over the head of a leaping figure.

In my peripheral vision I see

Martin Bent, hunched over his worktable,
overly intent on an empty piece of paper.

"Hey, Martin, know anything about this?"

"Nope," Martin answers, his eyes never
moving from the blankness spread out
on the table before him.

"You sure, Martin?"

"Yup," he replies,
eyes still focused downward.

"Sure was a lot of work."

"Yup," he responds once more
in robot fashion.

"It really is quite artistic," I say.
"Look at this detailed line
and intricate shading.
Someone put a lot of time into this."

Martin slowly lifts his head
and glances sideways toward the screen.

And with one deft move, I click

and scroll and lightly touch
the delete key and the picture
before us vanishes.

Erasing a picture is easy;
Erasing an attitude is not.

♦ ♦ ♦ ♦ ♦ ♦ ♦ ♦ ♦ ♦

April 8: Anger

Silas came into class today
and looked me square in the eyes
and called me
"timber nigger."

Inside I feel cold and hard
And in meanness,
I look Silas square in the eyes
and in my mind call him
farmer nigger.

♦ ♦ ♦ ♦ ♦

April 11: Resignation

Silas came into class today
and looked me square in the eyes
and called me
"timber nigger."

And I looked Silas square in the eyes
and said,
"Yes?"

♦ ♦ ♦

April 16: My Monthly Plea for Justice

Another school meeting tonight;
again I go
to see if those who make the rules
and set the tone,
who stare at me
with righteous indignation,
have finally understood.

I am told *timber nigger*
is not so bad.
I could have been called worse.

I am told this by adults,
who make decisions
for those who cannot think.

My brain fills with the possibilities
spread out before me like the paths
in a wood created by creatures

who live a life untrammeled by
hatred and bigotry.

What could be worse?

mountain nigger?
sand nigger?
sea nigger?

river nigger?
lake nigger?
plains nigger?

I am told *timber nigger*
is not so bad.
I could have been called worse.

I am told this by adults
who make decisions
for those who cannot think.

I think I know who cannot think.

♦ ♦ ♦ ♦ ♦ ♦ ♦ ♦ ♦ ♦ ♦ ♦

April 30: The Moment

The deafening silence filled the halls
as I entered the building this morning—
a deafening silence that clung to the walls;
tension, tension, tension,
mounted as the hours passed.

And now in the latter part of the afternoon,
Samuel Patterson stops me in the hall
between classes and pulls me aside.
And as he speaks
I catch my breath and hold it
hard inside my chest. He warns
me not to leave alone this afternoon,
but then he leaves and once again
I am alone in halls of mounting tension.

Jason Michaels and Maggie Brenden
and Frances Downey and Richard Green
all seek me out throughout the day.
One by one, they warn me not to be alone

and, one by one, they leave me all alone.

And so throughout the day I watch
and wait and watch and wait
so as not to be surprised,
not caught off guard,
full knowing that this could not be.

"We've had it, Evan Hill."

Startled by the volume of the voice,
I swing around and my eyes focus on
Martin Bent, bravely standing shoulder to
shoulder with Nathan Clark and Kyle Hawkins,
three "warriors" championing a cause,
ready to defend their misguided honor,
like royalty in some Greek tragedy
set on the banks of the Aegean Sea.
They are ready to kill the messenger, the one
who tells them what they do not wish to hear.
And there is Silas McAllister, lurking
        behind them
in shadow cast by the afternoon sun that
floods in through the cafeteria windows.

"Had what, Martin?" I respond softly
though my heart pounds as I glance
at this wall of shoulders, like a tsunami
in slow motion, moving closer, ready to

drown me in a sea of hate and anger.

"You gotta leave us alone, Evan."

Me
leave
them
alone?

Their ironic comment almost causes
me to smile but at the last moment
I hold my face suspended
lest the humor be viewed
as mockery which at this moment
is not a prudent option.

Had they heard my heart pounding
in my chest, they surely would have
seized the moment and capitalized
on my certain vulnerability.

"You gotta leave us alone, Evan."

The calm in Martin's voice contrasts
sharply with the movement of his body
shifting back and forth as he stands before me,
drawing my eyes downward where in horror
they rest on his left hand, which holds in

menacing grip a pair of metal scissors.

And for one brief moment
I entertain the thought of reason.
But I must dismiss it,
for surely one could find no reason
in existence here.

And just as I am feeling all is doomed,
I hear a voice come booming from behind,
and such a voice was never welcomed more.

"Hey, guys, what's up?" a voice inquires.

I then turn to verify the voice,
the holder, who with heavy tools in hand,
was headed down the hall to make repair.
He stops and nods and in his eyes,
I see, if not someone who gives support,
at least someone who understands that
something here is wrong. And I am
grateful for his appearance—
a barrier whose reef put up a shield
against the wave of anger and of hate,
to guard me as I move away
down the hall and down the stairs
and swiftly out the door.

♦ ♦ ♦ ♦ ♦ ♦ ♦ ♦

May 1: Dread

"Evan," my mother calls once more,
her voice echoing in my ears
as I pull the pillow over my head,
ostrichlike, hoping to have
the day evaporate before me
in a sea of sleep.
Is my courage fading?
Has my will been washed away
by the overflowing torrent of ignorance?

I have not yet spoken of yesterday
to my mother or even to my father;
I have not yet chosen to share with them
the anxious moments of the afternoon.
And in the quiet evening when my mother,
sensing something wrong, asked pointedly
about my day, I spoke of tests in math
and lab reports and even English essays,
but not of anger or of hate or fear.

And as she eyed me quite suspiciously,
I knew the look she gave said she inferred
something more.
The sea of information I had given
gave me away with massive certainty,
for though I often shared with them my day,
it rarely had the depth I had just conveyed.
But probing is not something she pursues,
and I was left alone.

Although they share my heart
and stand behind me in my cause,
I do not want their worry or their fear.
And so I did not tell them what
had happened yesterday.

Like the calm we feel before a storm,
I spent the night just waiting for the dawn.
And now that morning is here I must decide
to rise and meet the storm full force or not,
knowing that I dare not stay at home,
knowing that I must confront the force.
I pull my head from underneath my shroud
and rise and sigh and so begin my day.

♦ ♦ ♦ ♦ ♦ ♦ ♦ ♦ ♦ ♦ ♦ ♦ ♦ ♦

May 3: The Calm

Quiet,
all too quiet
for three days,
just quiet.

No slurs
no taunts
no whoops
no spit on my locker
no confrontations in the hall
no timber nigger name-calling
no silent glares across the room
no hostile gestures made.

Quiet,
all too quiet.

For three days,
just quiet.

Too quiet.

♦ ♦ ♦ ♦

May 5: All Things Great and Small

Who will tell my brother?
Who will tell him
that the fear, the hatred, the cruelty
were not kept for him or me
or for my mother or my father,
but shared with a creature that had no part
in its own undoing?

When we left for church this morning,
I should have sensed the ominous foreboding
that hung in the quiet air.
No one noticed that Butch was not asleep
in his usual place on the back porch,
protecting our domain
in his canine slumber.

And when we returned, eager for our coffee,
shared with morning paper and quiet conversation,
no one noticed our protector's absence
from the gravel drive.
But when my mother, heading to her garden,

with seed and a spade
to work in the afternoon sun,
rounded the back corner of the barn
hidden by lilac bushes in full bloom,
we heard a mournful cry.

My father flew from the house
with me in close pursuit.
I could not think what might have caused
my mother's cry of pain.

And when we came upon the scene,
I knew there could have been no clue
to the sight we saw before us.

My mother,
on her knees in bloody grass,
cradled Butch's head in her lap
and sobbed.

My father, crouching beside her,
one arm around her shoulders,
the other holding himself up from the ground,
suddenly seemed to lose the strength,
the calm, the stability
on which I had depended
so many times.
And I stared in disbelief

at the bloody carcass left
to speak the words of hate,
cowardly left for us to find.
I stared in disbelief.

Beneath my mother's arm, which
cradled my brother's childhood friend,
beneath my mother's arm which
shook uncontrollably with grief and horror
was a small
paper
feathered
headband.

Who will tell my brother
that the fear, the hatred, the cruelty
were not kept for him or me
or for my mother or my father,
but shared with a creature that had no part
in its own undoing?
Who will tell my brother?

♦ ♦ ♦ ♦ ♦ ♦ ♦ ♦ ♦ ♦

May 6: The Phone Call

I place the phone back in its cradle
and look at my mother as she
stands in the doorway,
worried and hurt.

"It's done," I say.

She turns away to seek my father out,
to console and to be consoled;
My mother, who does not share
her grief with others well,
now grieves in volumes,
not just for a guiltless pet,
but for her husband, her sons,
and for a whole nation of peoples.

The mournful silence
at the other end of the phone,
told me that my brother

could not fully comprehend,
the act of hate that had stripped
him of his childhood friend.

My brother Jacob knew
the day would come when Butch,
aging every hour, would no longer
greet him on the gravel drive,
but to lose this childhood protector
to hatred, to fear, to cruelty
was beyond his comprehension.

I told him how the police had come,
had seen this crime of hate,
and shook their heads in wonder.
I told him how they, paperwork in hand,
admitted no one likely would be blamed.

Jacob did not blame me.
Jacob would not blame me.
He knew that I had only carried on
the task that he had started in years past,
a task that had become
a matter of honor,
a matter of respect.

But I blamed me.

And so when Butch was buried in the backyard,
near the lilac bush in full spring bloom,
a prayer of thankfulness,
honoring his selfless sacrifice,
was sent respectfully with his spirit,
sent into the heavens with humble apology.

♦ ♦ ♦ ♦ ♦ ♦ ♦ ♦ ♦ ♦ ♦ ♦ ♦ ♦ ♦ ♦

May 7: Enlightenment

Though neither my mother
nor my father
nor I
told anyone of the act of hatred,
when I returned to school today,
everyone seemed to know:
the murmurs, the whispers,
the sideways glances
shot across the classroom.

And so I am not surprised at
Silas's approach as I sit alone
in the cafeteria eating my lunch.

"Hey, Evan," Silas calls,
"I hear Injuns eat dog meat;
did you eat yours?"

And so I know that those culpable,

so full of shameful pride,
must have boasted, must have bragged,
and I wonder if they thought
that they were counting coup.

I rise from the table, lifting my tray
with one hand. In one swift movement
I dump the contents into the bin behind me
and throw the plastic tray onto the shelf above.

And if I truly thought that Silas were to blame,
I would grab his throat
and choke him 'til he passed out on
the cold tile floor of the cafeteria
where we now stand face to face.

But patience has been taught me well,
and though inwardly I rage,
seemingly beyond control,
my restraint is still intact.

Silas is a man of words,
not deeds.
Silas could never have done
this premeditated act of hate.
Silas easily abuses with insults.
But Silas is a coward and though
he might glory in acts of violence

performed by others,
his passion would end there.

And as I suck my breath in slowly,
my teeth clenched behind
my tightened lips, I consciously hold
back the hateful words which are spewing
forth from my brain.

And as I stand here with my fists clenched,
my body frozen in anger,
I find myself surrounded.

"Easy, Evan," I hear in calm and somber tones,
and Jason Michaels soon is by my side.

"Ignore him, Evan," a voice behind me speaks
as Richard Green with glaring eyes steps forth.

"He's not worth it," adds Frances Downey,
who, with Maggie Brenden,
has suddenly appeared.

And soon I am surrounded by protectors,
protecting me more from myself than
from the Silases slowly gathering behind him.
And soon I realize how Butch,
Jacob's protector in life,

has indeed become my protector
in death.
His horrific death has galvanized
a circle of protectors,
who had been supportive in spirit
but indifferent in action,
who now have seen the truth,
have finally understood that
to be indifferent is to promote,
perhaps even accept, the hate.

And so throughout the day,
my circle of protectors moves with me,
bodyguards of friendship who
allow no stare to occur,
allow no comment to be made,
allow no hostile gesture to take place.

And, finally, I am not alone.

And, for the first time in many months,
when I return home from school,
my mother sees me smile.

♦ ♦ ♦ ♦ ♦ ♦ ♦ ♦ ♦

May 14: A Matter of Honor

Let it be resolved that from this day forth, in honor
of the heritage of this area, the Indian profile will
continue to be the official mascot of this school.

I could have understood
had they chosen to ignore me,
had they refused to pass my request—
that, officially, a ban be placed
upon the images, the profiles,
the logos that seemed to so defile
an entire race of peoples.

They could have done this
and I might have accepted it.

I would have accepted
that change in life is hard when
what you have had
is all you ever will have.

I could have accepted this and understood.

Instead, they chose to reaffirm
their ignorance, to sanction intolerance,
to proudly proclaim they have the right
to be intolerant.

And so they passed their own resolution.

They had sat for months,
sometimes with patience, mostly not,
while I proposed a resolution.
And in one spiteful moment,
they produced and passed their own.

♦ ♦ ♦ ♦ ♦ ♦ ♦ ♦ ♦ ♦ ♦ ♦ ♦ ♦

May 15: The Loss

"Well, we got it back, Evan,
we got it back," sneers Silas
as he edges up beside me
at my locker this morning,
looking pleased with himself
as though he alone has saved
his school from some horrendous loss.

"Got what, Silas?" I ask innocently
as though I have no inkling
of the cause for his insistence.

"We got our mascot back,"
he insists with eyes smirking,
not of pride for having been
a keeper of tradition,
but with eyes which taunt victory,
flaunting what he perceives to be my failure.

"You never lost it, Silas."

I turn to my locker, placing
my books on the shelf at eye level,
staring into the darkness before me.
It is an abyss of cold metal,
a darkness before me,
a darkness all around me.

Sensing another presence by my side,
whose coldness is far more pervasive
than Silas's taunting boasts, I close my
locker door and turn to face
a darkness filled with far more danger
than ever to be found in Silas.

"It's over, Evan; we won and you lost."
The words were uttered slowly.
The voice was deep and quiet.

And quite unlike my view of Silas,
I know full well that Martin knows
what this has been about,
and what is cold
and what is dark
and what is dangerous
is that Martin does not care.

"No, Martin, we've all lost."

♦ ♦ ♦ ♦ ♦ ♦ ♦ ♦ ♦

June 5: Awards Night

"Evan Hill."

As my name is called again,
for the seventh time,
I ease myself once more from the row
and climb over the sea of tangled legs
and auditorium seats that are spaced
too closely together for legs that grow
almost monthly. These are the legs of
senior friends, who clap me on the back
and spawn high fives,
gleeful in my accomplishments,
sharing in the thrill of victory,
if not in a common goal
to eradicate the injustices of the world,
at least in our shameless effort to show
the Martin Bents,
the Silas McAllisters,
the Lisa Kendalls
that we are the thinkers and doers.

We are willing and ready and anxious
to wallow in our pride.

And so before the night is through,
my pile of honors grows much
in height and depth;

I feel redemption
and gratitude to those who
willingly acknowledge who I am,
and my understanding of myself increases.

I am ready now to move ahead.
And though those so entrenched
in narrow-mindedness might never
find a path through the darkness,
others, who now send the message
that they have seen my hope,
confirm my faith in all humanity.

And so my friends, my protectors,
my quasi-converts, and I
all share our joys together.
With each name announced,
we join in shameless celebration,
cheering and clapping,
each one for the other.

We are willing and ready and anxious
to wallow in our pride.

♦ ♦ ♦ ♦ ♦ ♦ ♦ ♦ ♦

June 14: The Plan

Sitting quietly at supper,
my father slowly stirs his soup,
waiting for it to cool, listening solemnly
as my mother asks about my day.

My father and I can sense each other's
thoughts—he has no need to ask;
he knows my strength
and I know his,
and like the old brown backpack
hanging on the wall in the attic
he carries both his weight and mine.

It is always my mother,
who worries so about my inner pain,
who wonders if the burden I have
taken on is much too heavy.
It is always my mother,
protective of her cub,

who asks about my day.
"Evan?" My mother says,
seeing that my thoughts have,
once again, traveled off.

I tell her of the words I heard
throughout the halls today as both
friend and foe spread the words
like chemicals in a farmer's field,
hoping both to kill and cultivate,
spread the words,
leaked the plan,
the plan to assert their rights.

I tell my mother and my father
of a plan to make a banner,
with a painted face,
and vacant eyes,
and an ornate headdress.
It is to be proudly carried
onto the field behind the leaving seniors
who, on their day of commencement,
will then have a memory of their past
to carry with them.

I tell my mother and my father of the plan
and how so many wish it would not be;
and that many are not proud to be
a part of a plan that leaves such a memory.

I tell them how I tried to stop this plan.

But others have the right;

and so our rights are stripped.

And so it will take place.

♦ ♦ ♦ ♦ ♦ ♦ ♦ ♦ ♦

June 22: Graduation

Pulling into the parking lot,
I see before me a sea of faces,
waiting, looking to see what I will say.

But I know what is waiting before me,
warned by those who thought it wrong,
taunted by those who claimed the right.

When my mother and father and I
discussed the situation three nights ago,
we all agreed that now was not the time,
not the place, not the moment to confront
the spitefulness of those who claim the
right to flaunt an Indian face on an old sheet
mounted between two poles, an Indian face
with irisless eyes and war-painted cheeks,
framed with red and yellow feathered headdress.

And there it is, in all its sad spitefulness,

temporarily sagging against the fence,
waiting for its moment of glory.

I arrive early, to take my place among
the graduates, among those who have been
my classmates for what seems all eternity,
and there it is.

Maggie Brenden is the first to greet me:

"Evan, Evan, what are we going to do?"

The "we" she said rings loudly in my head.
And there I stand, not alone, but one
among many who gather at one end
of the field, wondering what should be done.

"Nothing," I reply, "we'll do nothing."

The murmuring among my comrades
echoes the dissent I feel in my own heart,
but as the group around me grows,
I know I have won. What began as one
is one no longer, and no banner
meant to spite our thoughts
has power any longer.
This banner has united us
and gratitude I feel.

Many, who have not shared my belief
that a picture could hurt a people,
now understand that this has never been
about a picture, but about respect
and knowing who we truly are.

I look across the field and see my family,
my father and mother and brother,
taking their seats in the stadium,
chatting with friends and neighbors,
and wonder if they see or sense my pride.

And then my mother catches my glance and
with a small wave and a slight nod,
I give her the assurance that she needs,
that calm and graciousness will host the day.

And then I see my father smiling down
and know that he approves my very being,
that nothing I can do will disappoint
and all that I am is part of him.

In single file we march in proud solemnity
across the field to rows of chairs,
two hundred chairs awaiting us,
waiting for us to put our childhood lives
behind and move into our futures,
but I feel that I have already moved into

my future; I have already seen my destiny;
I have chosen my path. And now I move
into the front-row aisle seat, and I think
how appropriate. For almost a year now
I have felt so much in front, but always
        on the edge.

Ceremonially, we all stand and sit and speak
and listen to the speeches, the proclamations,
the presentations, going forward one by one to
claim a document which sends us forth,
        educated,
into the world, out of the past, into the future.

And as this solemn rite approaches its end,
and we all stand in unison to sing
our alma mater in one solid voice,
an elbow, nudging sharply at my side,
catches me off guard.

"*Psst*, Evan, look," Maggie whispers.

Moving awkwardly, across the field,
comes the banner
weaving and wobbling,
held unsteadily by two young boys,
one barely five feet tall, the other six feet two,
brothers of two senior classmates who, proudly,

worked for days plotting, planning, painting
     this creation,
two young men to carry on this new tradition,
to flaunt their ignorance on such a day of pride.

And as the cheers erupt from the crowd
and clapping from the throng behind me grows,
a sight takes place that fills my heart with joy,
a sight that tells me what I've done is right.

A rippling takes place and as I turn,
I see the movement grow,
to left and right, throughout the row in front,
as one by one some classmates sit,
remove their caps and place them in their laps
and bow their heads in clear acknowledgement
that what they witness
does not make them proud.

And in surprise the claps and cheers grow less
as some here wonder at this sad response.
And though in numbers we perhaps are few,
I know we send a message loud and clear:
we now leave legacy of our own,
that we have done our part
to show the world
that hate and shameful pride
must cease to be.

♦ ♦ ♦ ♦ ♦ ♦ ♦

Epilogue

As I walk across the college campus,
in the evening shadows of the White Mountains
still green with the lushness of summer,
I find myself comfortable in my surroundings,
accepted by my peers, a newfound family,
native peoples from places near and far.
Will they become part of me, and I of them?
I find myself taken into the fold of those
who understand and know what it is like
to see through different eyes,
to know what it is like to be seen by hostile eyes.

We come together
to let the world see who we are,
to let the world see that we are people with histories,
with similar, but different histories,
to let the world see that we are people with feelings,
with similar, but different feelings.

I know my struggle is not over.
It is a struggle which will continue
as long as people see others as different.
But I know I have made a difference.
And I know I am no longer alone.

♦ ♦ ♦ ♦ ♦ ♦ ♦ ♦ ♦ ♦ ♦ ♦ ♦

In recent years, the practice of using American Indian mascots and team names in schools has drawn protests across the country by people who consider the mascots insensitive. More than six hundred colleges and high schools have changed their mascots in response. There are at least 135 high schools in New York State alone that still have Indian mascots or team names. This story is a fictionalized account of the real-life experiences of the author's two sons.